When Faith Has Conquered Fear

Written by:

Christopher C. Smith

Christopher C. Smith

**Father, Author, Actor, Song Writer, Independent Book
& Movie Publisher**

Thank you's & Dedications

First I would like to give thanks to God

My Beautiful Mother
Ora Henderson

My Beautiful Daughter
Lauren Madison Smith

My Supportive A.O.D Family

Sponsored By

Table of Contents

Table of Contents 7

Chapter 1 8

Chapter 2 17

Chapter 3 31

Chapter 4 42

Chapter 1

As the whistle blew loudly because of a foul, I couldn't help but acknowledge that the adrenaline rush and hype were building throughout the stadium. I knew this was it, or should I say, it was either do or die. The shot clock wound down to seconds in the championship game—the last game of the season.

"Two shots," the ref called. As both teams lined up for the free throws, my friend Keith Hunter prepared to shoot his foul shots.

While looking down and saying a prayer, I heard a thump as the first attempt missed. I walked slowly over to Keith and whispered in his ear, "Take your time. You got this." Not knowing what was going to happen, in my mind, I quickly tried to draw up a play and come to a conclusion, as if something wrong was going to happen or the ball was going to end up in the other team's hands. I began to hear a severe rumbling in my stomach as if the coca tea and large pizza I had devoured before the game wasn't sitting well—like it was going to come up one way or another.

Before he could even take the shot, I looked over to the crowd and couldn't help but notice my beautiful fiancée Malaya cheering while holding up a sign with my and my friend Keith's name written in graffiti letters along with cool decorations around it. This was a shock to me because during the regular season, she barely even spoke to any of my friends or teammates. I didn't think much of it, but I turned and looked at Keith to see if he had noticed it. To my surprise, it looked as if he did, and within seconds, he blew a slight kiss to her before taking the second foul shot.

Thummmmp! The basketball bounced off the backboard to me in slow motion, like a sign that I was to be the hero and save the game. With no hesitation I quickly ran and made my way through the driving lane before anyone else could notice. To even my surprise, I jumped high enough for the rebound and slam dunk as the horn that finalized the game blew. The crowd erupted as I made my way down from the rim. But somehow I landed awkwardly. As my teammates came and jumped on me in excitement, I felt a sharp pain in my lower leg and screamed for help.

"Help! Help!" I yelled. I tried to push off the remaining teammates that were left celebrating on top of me as I gripped my leg. I was helped off the courts while the announcers were still celebrating and talking about how important this game was to me, knowing there were scouts all over looking to recruit for their semiprofessional basketball team. "Hey, good job," "Nice work," "You're up next," is all I repeatedly heard as I geared up to head to the hospital to see what exactly I had injured. I was still in pain, and my mind was racing at a hundred miles per hour with thoughts of the terrible career-ending injuries I had heard of other athletes suffering.

As I prepped myself to go on a stretcher, there was a slight tap on my shoulder. As I turned to my right, still in pain, I couldn't help but cheer up a bit. It was my friend Keith.

"Hey, you really saved us out there. I had no idea how bad I was going to fold under pressure while shooting those free throws. My mind was all over the place. But then you flew out of nowhere and put the ball back in the rim the way you did. You are truly a lifesaver."

"Ah, no problem," I replied as I gently smiled, trying not to show the pain I was in and how much what he said meant me. I wanted to ask about my girl and the whole kiss-blowing thing, but as I began to fix my lips to speak, I was quickly hauled off in the ambulance and rushed to the hospital. Lying in my hospital bed, it seemed like forever and a day before I was attended to. I couldn't help but start to break down as tears heavily filled my eyes and poured down my cheeks. "Why, God? Why me?" I asked repeatedly. It seemed stuff like this only happened to me.

Amid my emotional outburst, I heard a somewhat deep voice say, "Hey, are you okay, bud?"

Trying not to show my tears, I quickly wiped my face and blew my nose. "Hi, my name is Mohammed," I said, trying my best to cheer up. Before he could even finish his sentence of introducing himself, just by the badge, I knew his name and that he was the doctor that would be seeing me. "You must be Dr. Wallace?"

"Ha ha," he replied with a small smirk on his face. "Indeed I am. I will be your doctor for the time you are here, but first, we will need to run tests to see what exactly is wrong."

I began to explain what had happened, but he quickly cut me off as he started to read a piece of paper that was attached to his clipboard.

I couldn't help but notice the concerned look on his face. "Is everything okay?" I asked.

"Hmmm," he replied with a more serious but kind of confused facial expression. "I see that you have a sports injury, and because of that, you are required to take a drug test."

"A what!" I replied, looking more puzzled than ever. I'd never heard of that. "What for?" I asked. "Can you please explain?"

"Well, For many different things," Dr. Wallace replied as he ran through a list of reasons drug testing is necessary. "Are you on any medications or have you taken any illegal substances within the last seventy-two hours?"

I knew for a fact I had never in my life done or been addicted to any type of substance. With a serious look on my face, I quickly responded, "No! But, okay, that's fine," I said, knowing I didn't smoke, drink, or take any other type of drugs.

Chapter 2

After taking both my X-ray and drug test, I dozed off, only to wake up to an entire crowd all around me, including my mom, my coaches, and what looked to be recruiters.

"Is everything okay?" I asked as I noticed a tear coming down both my girlfriend's and mom's faces. I noticed that the medication they had placed me on made me feel exhausted.

"You know, you're a hero, Son," my mom said with joy, "with what you did and how you saved the game. Shortly after you were carried away, a few news reporters asked if you're alright and when you'll get back to normal. Without a doubt, I quickly assured them on your behalf that you will be out in no time."

"Oh, wow, Mom," I said with a gentle but sarcastic reply. "No, you're right. I'll be out of here in no time and back on the court." Trying to embrace the moment and finish my sentence, I couldn't help but notice the team of doctors and a guy in a nice clean suit come rushing in. They began to talk, and with a quick glance, I noticed Dr. Wallace was in no mood for games. I couldn't help but notice the tension in the room. The vibe had gotten thrown way off. Dr. Wallace then stepped up with no hesitation. As he began his speech, I knew it wasn't good, just from his tone.

"Ahem" he began, clearing his throat and barely making eye contact with me. "The staff here and I all have a couple of questions."

I felt my heart began to pound at an extremely high rate. I took a deep breath and replied, "Go ahead and tell me what's wrong."

"Sir, before the game, did you take any enhancement drugs or drinks that you might have thought would have helped you in today's game?"

"No," I said as everyone in the room, including me, was shocked and stunned. The doctors continued this line of questioning. Each question was more hurtful than the last, knowing they would think I would do something like that and risk my career.

Dr. Wallace then took the spotlight again to inform us that something was wrong—very wrong. "Well, your leg injury isn't that serious; it's just a minor sprain. But I'm sad to say your drug test brought up a couple of things."

I knew it was going downhill from there. "Like what?" I asked as tears began to fill my eyes. I couldn't help but notice my mom was in sudden shock. Her eyes were filled with tears.

Dr. Wallace began to read off what was found in my system. "First, sir, we found cocaine."

"COCAINE!" I yelled at the top of my lungs in full disbelief. "How so? I wouldn't even know where to get it, let alone use it before a game."

"Calm down, Mr. Mohammed. I feel your pain. I mean, think back, was it mixed with anything, or did you eat or drink anything today or the night before? Because it is possible you did and weren't aware."

"Well, sir, to be honest, all I had was a large pizza and a large glass of coca tea, but that's about it."

With a shocked look on his face, Dr. Wallace asked, "What was it that you had to drink again?"

Repeating myself, I firmly said, "A large glass or two of coca tea."

"Well, medically speaking, there are foods and drinks we put in our body that may trigger or cause a false-positive test result, and I believe that is what triggered one of the things that was found in your system."

With the most confused look on my face, I couldn't help but ask for more details.

"See, drinking coca tea could lead to a false-positive result for cocaine. The tea is popular in South America and is made from the leaves of the coca plant, the same source from which cocaine is derived. In a 2006 study, five people drank coca tea before undergoing a drug test. All of the participants tested positive for cocaine metabolites two hours after consuming the tea, and three participants still tested positive for cocaine after thirty-six hours. The researchers concluded that healthcare professionals should consider a history of coca tea ingestion when interpreting urine toxicology results."

"Wow." Everyone in the room was shocked that something so simple could cause such false results.

"But, Doctor, you said two things were found. What was the second?"

He replied, "A high volume of liquor."

"Liquor?" I shouted as my voice then reached an ultimate high peak. "How so? I don't believe this! I don't drink at all."

As I began to break down and cry, Dr. Wallace explained why eating a large amount of pizza was actually bad for us. "You could possibly fail a breathalyzer test after consuming yeasty foods, according to the BBC. Yeast ferments sugars into alcohol, which is why your test result could possibly come back positive. Another Thing

z we eat that may also make you fail a drug test is poppy seeds. Poppy seeds naturally contain the compounds morphine and codeine, so consumption of some products with poppy seeds can trigger false-positive results for these drugs. A 1987 study shows that five members of a lab baked cookies containing about one teaspoon, or five milliliters, of a poppy seed filling that
they bought from the grocery store. Two hours after eating several cookies, all of the lab members tested positive for opiates. The concentration of the drug was greater than three hundred nanograms per milliliter, which was the minimum cutoff used by the test. In 1998, the Department of Health and Human Services

changed the cutoff to two thousand nanograms per milliliter in order to avoid false-positive results from eating poppy seeds, according to a 2008 review study. However, most laboratories continue to use lower cutoffs."

As doctor Wallace went on about the things I had eaten and how they could possibly ruin my career, I couldn't help but listen and learn more about how even certain soaps used in hospitals to wash babies shortly after birth could cause the infants to test positive for marijuana on some newborn screening tests, which are done to determine if a mother was using drugs while pregnant.

"According to a 2012 study, health care workers figured out that babies who are washed with soaps including Johnson & Johnson's Head-to-Toe Baby Wash, J & J Bedtime Bath, CVS Night-Time Baby z Bath, Aveeno Soothing Relief Creamy Wash, and Aveeno Wash Shampoo tested positive on a urine drug screening test for THC, the active compound in marijuana. The researchers in that study said they aren't sure why the soaps cause a false positive. It could be that some of the compounds in the soap have a structure that is partly similar to THC, or it could be that chemicals in the soap change the way the test works. As for how the soap got into the urine sample, the researchers suspect that some residual soap on the babies' skin washed off into their urine samples."

After about an hour of discussion, as Dr. Wallace was winding down and getting ready to leave, a few tall guys with gray suits walked in and introduced themselves.

"Hi, my name is Michael. I am the chief executive of the Smithville Semi-Pro Basketball League, and we have been watching you for quite some time. You are an extremely talented guy with a bright future. But—"

"But what?" I interrupted, knowing where all this was headed knowing that I just tested positive for all those drugs. I knew it couldn't get any worse, and my heart began to pound even more by the second just looking at these men's faces along with everyone else's in the room. I couldn't help but tear up as I then repeatedly asked, "But what . . . but what?"

Then and there my whole world started crashing down on me as the very words I never wanted to hear in my life came out of Michael's mouth.

"Because of your recent test results, you have been banned from playing in our league!"

"No," I yelled. I cried, hitting my fist along the bed as everyone, including my mom and girlfriend Malaya, tried to calm me down. "Nooooo! You can't do this to me. This can't be happening!"

The men lowered their heads and began to walk out of the hospital room.

Chapter 3

"Ahh." I took a deep breath after finally being released from the hospital. I was back to walking—well, not completely, but better than I was when I was admitted. While still using crutches, I wobbled and hopped right into my car. It wasn't until I put my key in the ignition and looked over that I found a gang of text messages and voicemails on my phone. Some were from friends and family, and some were from my friend and teammate Keith and younger cousin Cory. They all said I should try moving on and go out with them for a few drinks and laughter—just for one night.

I thought to myself, "After all I've been through these last few days, the opportunity does seem well overdue." Within seconds, I replied that I was down.

"Cool," Keith said. "Get fly. I will be at your house shortly."

Without hesitation, I quickly got in the shower and got dressed. Then I sat quietly in my living room, nervous, waiting to get the call or text that he was pulling up. For some strange reason, I kept getting the feeling that something crazy was going to happen or that I shouldn't be going out. I tried to talk myself out of it. "Hey, you only live once." It'd been a while since I really hung out, and I knew this would help me get my mind off things.

I paced the floor and practiced approaching peopleso I could fit in and not seem like an oddball. That's when I got the call from Keith that he was about to pull up.

Shortly after making my way to the front door, I again had that feeling that I was supposed to stay in. But for some strange reason, I ignored the voice in my head and swiftly made my way to the car. Keith and I greeted each other happily as if we hadn't seen each other in years.

"Am I dressed right for where you are taking me?"

"Yes," Keith said while trying to keep himself from busting out in laughter. "Don't worry, kiddo. I got you. I will make sure this is the time of your life."

"So, what's the plan?" I asked. "So I can be prepared."

"Plan for what?" Keith quickly replied. "Just relax and have fun."

"Oh boy," I thought to myself. Then I sat back and relaxed and let the breeze from the wind flow through my hair. I tried to forget the fact that somehow I had to make something of myself, knowing I just got the boot from the basketball league for eating the wrong foods.

"Make a turn onto Smithville Boulevard," Keith's loud GPS stated. From the directions given, I knew we were close to where we were going, and by the name mentioned, I could tell it was a bar.

"Um, hey, Keith, you know I don't drink, right?"

"Yeah, don't worry. Just try it. A shot or two won't hurt anybody."

Feeling peer pressured, I finally gave in. "What the heck! It's just this one time, and it's about time I really start living." We finally made it to our destination, and as we found our way inside, the music blasted loud in my ear. I would be lying if I said that it didn't make me jump just a little.

"Hey, what's up?" Keith stopped to speak to everyone he passed. I could tell he must be a regular here, as people were calling him by his full name and nickname. After finally finding a seat, we were approached by a waiter. To my surprise, it was our other teammate Joey.

"Hey, sorry for what happened. I heard the news about the whole drug-testing thing."

I sighed and took a deep breath, thinking I was going to forget all about it. It would be a lie to say that it didn't just open up a closed door that I wasn't ready to speak about. While trying to maintain my composure, I responded, "Yeah, well, it's all God's plan. You know I will come back eventually to order our food and drinks."

*****

Looking at the time, I saw it was starting to get late. I knew I had important things to do the next day, but I was really catching a vibe, dancing all over the dance floor to about every song the DJ had played from all types of genres. I had put my phone on silent so I could enjoy myself with no interruptions.

As the liquor and shots that Keith had ordered finally kicked in, more so for Keith than me, he began to get more emotional by the minute. Every line was, "Hey, you know I love you for life, my bro."

All my replies were, "Yeah, bro, I know you're drunk. Sit down." I tried hard not to laugh, trying to be serious.

"Hey, bro, guess what?" Keith asked. The more he spoke, the more I could smell the liquor on his breath.

"What's that?" I replied as I assumed he was going to tell me that he loved me and he had my back for life for the thousandth time. But this time, as I was looking away, trying not to laugh at the look on his face, he turned my head toward his.

"No, no, no, bro, listen. There's something I got to tell you, and I just don't know how."

"Oh boy," I replied jokingly, thinking this still was some part of him playing games while being drunk.

"No, listen to me. I'm serious, no joke."

After he finally got my full attention, I couldn't help but notice that he really had to get something off of his chest.

"What's that, bro? Speak," I said, this time looking him right in the eyes with a much more serious tone.

"Look, I don't know how to say this, but you know your girl Malaya?"

"Yeah, what about her?" I replied, still thinking he was going to hit me with teasing, a joke, or something random that was going to end up in laughter. But for some strange reason, he didn't. He paused, trying to get his thoughts in order, all while trying to fight back his tears. I knew he was going to tell me something serious. While slurring his words and wiping the tears from his eyes before he took the final drink from his glass, he put his arm on my shoulder and said, "Remember when you were in the hospital after the game? She and I went back to your house and did something."

"What!" I yelled, swiping his arm off my shoulder as hard as I possibly could. "This all has to be a joke.

You're kidding me!" I was in disbelief, not wanting to believe the words that were coming out of my friend's mouth and the details he was spilling on how they had linked up numerous times behind my back.

He then laid the final dagger, the words that no man ever wanted to hear from his homie's mouth: she was three weeks pregnant and the baby might not be mine. As he tried to go on, I began to shed tears. I grabbed my things and began to call an Uber, all while texting and trying to get a hold of Malaya to see if what Keith had told me was true. I sent text after text with no reply, before she finally messaged me back and said, "Yes, I'm so sorry. I was waiting for the perfect time to tell you but didn't know when."

Still in shock, I paced back and forth trying to text her with my hands shaking. The Uber was taking forever. I didn't even want to see Keith ever again, let alone speak to him, but I knew I had to because he was my ride and there were no other options. I quickly snatched his car keys out of his hands, and still in shock I sped off, leaving him at the club and heading toward Malaya's house doing damn near 100 miles per hour in a 35 mph lane.

Chapter 4

I pushed my foot further and further down on the gas pedal as I sped toward Malayla's house. I couldn't help but have thoughts of my girlfriend and my best friend having sex flash in my head—let alone of her being pregnant and not telling me. For some reason, it felt like the more I thought about it, the faster I drove, hitting each block with sharp corners and barely even missing potholes. "How could she do this to me?" I screamed out loud while bursting into tears as the rage grew more and more. "Why me?" I asked repeatedly. I then began to ask myself a series of questions like, "What did I do wrong?"

"How could I be so blind to ignore the warning signs and red flags?" I felt like I could've at least been warned or told this face-to-face by her and not my friend/teammate who was drunk.

As the GPS began to speak, telling me I was five minutes away from my destination, I began to slow down. I still ignored the calls and texts from Keith to bring back his car. While reaching over to pick up my phone, for some reason I wasn't able to fully get a grasp on it, and it fell in between the seats. "Damn!" I yelled as I tried reaching over and grabbing it while still trying to keep my eyes on the road.

Suddenly, the weather changed, and before I knew it, it started to drizzle. Horns from other cars began honking, louder and louder, from me swerving through lanes, in and out, trying to get my phone. I was then blinded by a bright headlight, and the other driver met me head-on and crashed. Car parts and glass were everywhere, and the airbag had deployed. The other cars tried their hardest not to add on and swerve into the mess I had made. Still dazed while trying to undo my seat belt, I felt my face, which seemed to be bloody from the shattered glass. There was a small but painful bump on my forehead from me hitting my head on the steering wheel. I quickly unfastened my seat belt and made my way out of the car to see who and what exactly I had hit. "Are you okay?" one lady asked while watching from afar with a small group of people.

I looked at the car with a strange face because, for some reason, the car looked familiar. Still, it was hard for me to really get a glimpse of who was behind the wheel, so I began to walk closer and closer while yelling repeatedly, "Are you okay? Please say something." A soon as I glanced over to see through the window even closer, my jaw dropped in complete shock. To my surprise, it was my girlfriend, Malaya.

"Help! Help!" I yelled. "Someone please call the cops." Each time I yelled, screaming at the top of my voice, I began to feel weaker. Shortly after seeing my girlfriend lying there on the steering wheel, not moving, I erupted in tears. "Call the ambulance. Please, someone, please don't stand there." Without waiting any longer for assistance, I walked to the car and quickly unfastened her seat belt. I lifted her out of the car and carried her over to the sidewalk, holding her close. With both our blood dripping from my clothes and rain drizzling down my face, I started to break down and cry even more.

"I'm sorry, Malaya. This is all my fault. I'm so sorry. Please forgive me, please forgive me," I said, time after time. She then opened her eyes and realized it was me.

"It's okay," she said while coughing and straining her voice to speak. I could tell she was in a lot of pain and was just in shock like I was. "I'm sorry too," she said while breaking down in my arms. "I should have said something sooner, but I didn't want to distract you with your big game. I know how important it was to you, so I kept it all in. I hate that you had to find out this way."

"It's okay. If anything we will get the test done after we check to see if the baby is okay. But, Malaya, where were you headed?"

While wiping the tears from her eyes, she replied, "I felt bad, and I wanted to come and comfort you. I kept texting you to see exactly where you were. I just figured you couldn't be that far since you last called me."

The sirens became louder and louder while swarming around us, from cops, ambulances, and fire trucks. I couldn't help but notice the bright lights from flashlights coming toward us as the cops came to see exactly what had happened.

Shortly after explaining and giving a quick statement, because I admitted that I took a drink, I found myself being given a breathalyzer test, and the cops ordered me to walk in a straight line. After I passed all the tests given, one officer insisted,

"You're one lucky fella because you just missed the limit. Had you been over with such a mess here, I would have definitely put you in my back seat and charged you with a DUI."

"Oh man, thanks so much, Officer. I really appreciate it," I thanked him over and over.

"Ma'am, you look pretty bad—you both do. By any chance do you guys need any medical assistance?"

"Hmmm, no, we'll be just fine." We stood there with all these cops and now news reporters.

"Oh yeah, one last thing," the cop said as he looked at us both. I need you guys' license, insurance, and registration, please. Right then and there, it hit me as I remembered that the car I was driving was not mine.

"Omg, Keith," I said out loud while explaining to the cop that the car was not mine. And from then on out, the whole scene became very hostile. Before I knew it, I was being put in handcuffs and placed in the back of the officer's car. While the officers were still getting questions from Malaya, I couldn't help but sit there and realize that this was it—this really might be how this day ended. I couldn't help but think to myself that I really messed up this time around. With my hands cuffed behind my back and my head hitting repeatedly against the cop's headrest, I began to pray as I prayed like never before.

I heard a familiar voice scream my name, "Mohammed, Mohammed, where are you?" I instantly turned my head to see who it was. Without a doubt, it was Keith.

"Hey, where are you going?" I heard the officer yell firmly. You can't go over there; it's a crime scene.

Keith then explained the whole story, and I was released from the car and handcuffs. I hugged and held onto Keith while apologizing over and over. "It's okay," he told me, and we both broke down in tears. I could tell I had my guardian angels all around me because not only had I wrecked my girlfriend's and friend's car, but also the cops, for some reason, were being understandable with the whole thing, and I wasn't charged with anything.

As time went on and the scene began to clear up, I still didn't feel safe with my girl getting into an accident and being pregnant. I firmly suggested that she, too, get checked up on, at least for the baby's sake, and then we'd do the DNA test later. But as I really thought about it, with me being deeply in love with my girl and with my friend by my side, especially at a time like this, I really didn't care whose baby it was as long as he or she was healthy with five fingers and five toes.

Malaya agreed and was taken off in the ambulance shortly after. I apologized to Keith for acting the way I did and for taking his car and leaving him stranded. But with a confused look on my face, I looked at Keith and said, "How did you make it here and know

exactly where I was?"

To my surprise, Keith explained how he was able to find me from the tracking device that was attached to his phone through his app. He then called another friend to take him to the location.

While piling up and heading to the hospital, I couldn't help but thank Keith and apologize one last time. He, too, apologized for his actions, which triggered me to act the way did and caused all this. Shortly after, we made it to the hospital and were greeted by the doctor, who informed us that Malaya and the baby were doing just fine with no injuries at all.

Still covered in blood and thinking how this whole day had gone, I couldn't help but realize how blessed I truly
was. With the right people by my side, I knew I could get along in life and become something great. At that moment, I looked up, and to my surprise was a big poster about joining the military and the instructions on how to do so. I took it as a sign from God and quickly called the number. I never would have thought in a million years that I would be where I was today and would want to join the military. Still, I would do anything to protect my future wife and child.

While walking and making the appointment to meet with a recruiter, I knew it was my faith that had overcome the fear, allowing me to become who I was today. And without a doubt, I quickly said a small prayer, ending it with, "Thank you, God! Amen."

The End!